Written and designed by Annie Simpson
Illustrated by Clare Fennell

Copyright © 2011

make believe ideas ltd

The Wilderness, Berkhamsted, Herts, HP4 2AZ, UK.

www.makebelieveideas.com

Hickory Dickory Dock

Annie Simpson · Clare Fennell

make believe ideas

Hickory **dickory** dock,

the mouse **ran** up the ClocK.

The ClocK struck **one**,

the mouse ran down!

Hickory **dickory** dock.

Max ran **down** the ClocK,

acroSs the mat,

under the chair

and into the KitcHen,

where MummY MoUse was baking.

"But there's nothing to do," said Max.

"I'm sure you'll think of something," said Mummy Mouse.

"And tie your laces before you have an accident!"

But Max had a better idea...

Hickory **dickory** dock,

the mouse **swuNg** from the **CloCK.**

The **CloCK** struck **two**,

he lost his **shoe!**

Hickory **dickory** dock.

"Is Kevin here yet?"

asked Max.

"No, not yet,"

said Mummy Mouse.

"Why don't you go and tidy your room? And put your skates away – it's dangerous to leave them lying around!"

But Max had a better idea...

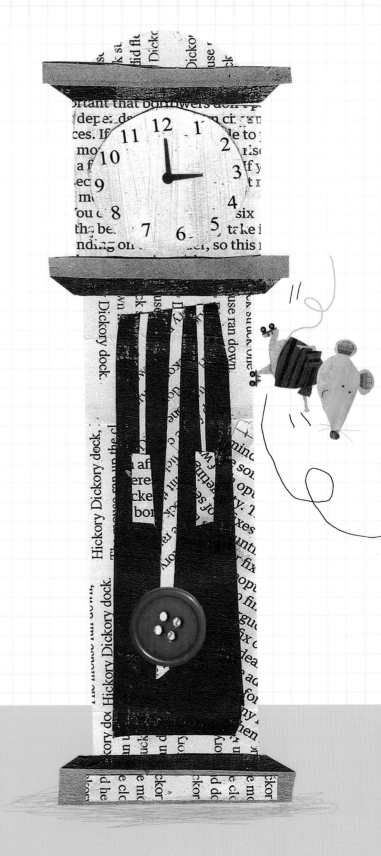

Hickory **dickory** dock,

Max **skated** down the Clock.

The Clock struck **three**,

he **baNged** his knee!

Hickory **dickory** dock.

"It's getting late. Do you think Kevin's got lost?"

asked Max.

"No, I don't think he's lost,"

said Mummy Mouse.

"I'm sure he'll be here any minute. Why don't you wait for him in the garden?"

But Max had a better idea...

the mouse **jumPed** off the CloCK.

The CloCK struck **four** – a **knock** at the door!

knock!
knock!

Hickory **dickory** dock.

"Kevin's here!"

said Max.

"Okay! Sit nicely
and do a
puzzle together,"

said Mummy Mouse.

But Max had a
better idea...

Hickory **dickory** dock,
the mice d**a**n**c**e**d** round the **ClocK**.
The **ClocK** struck **five**, they **jigged** and **jived!**
Hickory **dickory** dock.

"When will dinner be ready?"

asked Max.

"Soon, Max. Why don't you help me find some cherries for the top of the cake?"

said Mummy Mouse.

Max found the cherries. But then he had a better idea...

Hickory **dickory** dock,

Max **juggled**

on the ClocK.

The Clock struck six

as he did

faNcY

tRicKs!

Hickory

dickory

dock.

"Here they are, Mum!"

said Max.

"Thank you, Max,"

said Mummy Mouse.

"Now, put Kevin's bike in the garage, please – it looks like rain."

But Max had a better idea . . .

Hickory **dickory** dock,

they **cycLeD down** the ClocK.

The CloC**K** struck **seven**,

"Be **careful**, Kevin!"

Hickory
dickory
dock.

"We're hungry!"

said Max.

"You can't eat anything now – you'll spoil your dinner,"

said Mummy Mouse.

But Max had a better idea...

Hickory **dickory** dock,

"There's **cheese** under the ClocK!"

The ClocK struck **eight**,

they just

couldn't wait.

Hickory

dickory

dock.

"Mum, we're bored!"

said Max.

"Well, if you're looking for something to do, why don't you lay the table?"

said Mummy Mouse.

But Max had a better idea...

Hickory **dickory** dock,

they **climbed**

back up

the **Clock**.

The ClocK struck **nine** as they made a sign!

We want dinner!

Hickory

dickory

dock.

"Is it dinner time yet?"

asked Max.

"Not long now!
Just time for you to do
some colouring,"

said Mummy Mouse.

But Max had a
better idea...

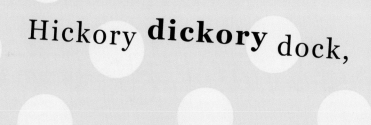

Hickory **dickory** dock,

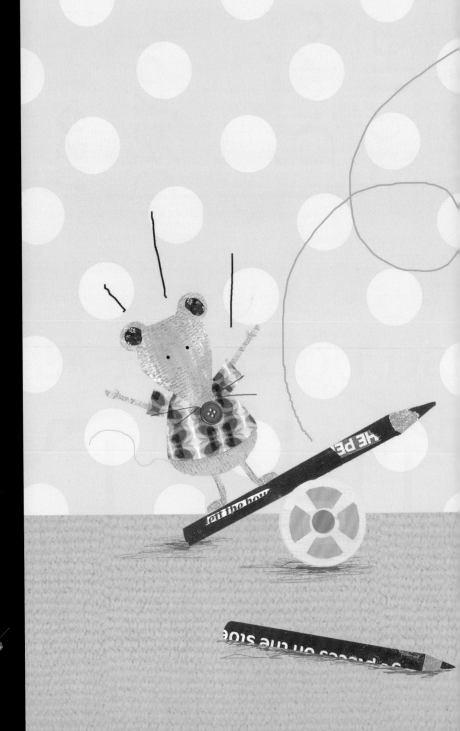

the mice **jumped** **over** the Clock.

The Clock struck **ten,**
"Let's **do it again!**"

Hickory **dickory** dock.

"Dinner time, boys! I've made cheese sandwiches, cheese pizza, cheese pancakes and cheese cake,"

said Mummy Mouse.

"Now, come and sit down."

And Max thought that was a great idea ...

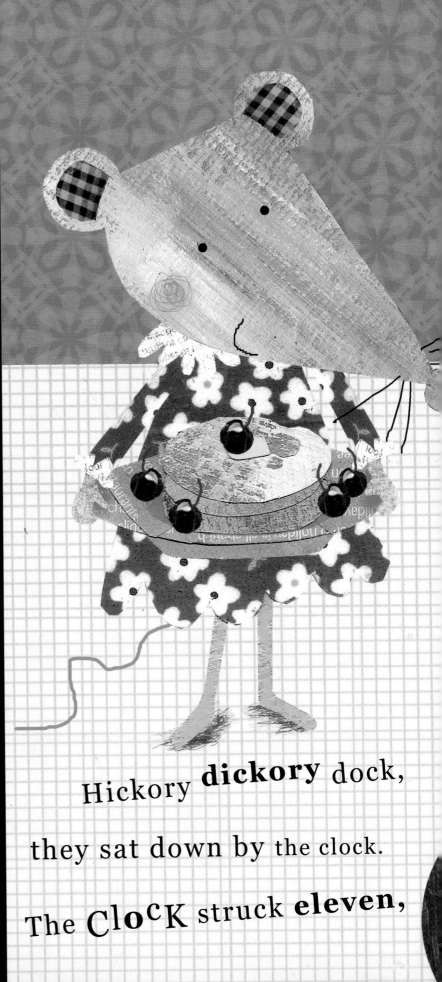

Hickory **dickory** dock,

they sat down by the clock.

The CloCK struck **eleven**,

"We're in **cheese** he**a**v**En**!"

Hickory **dickory** dock.

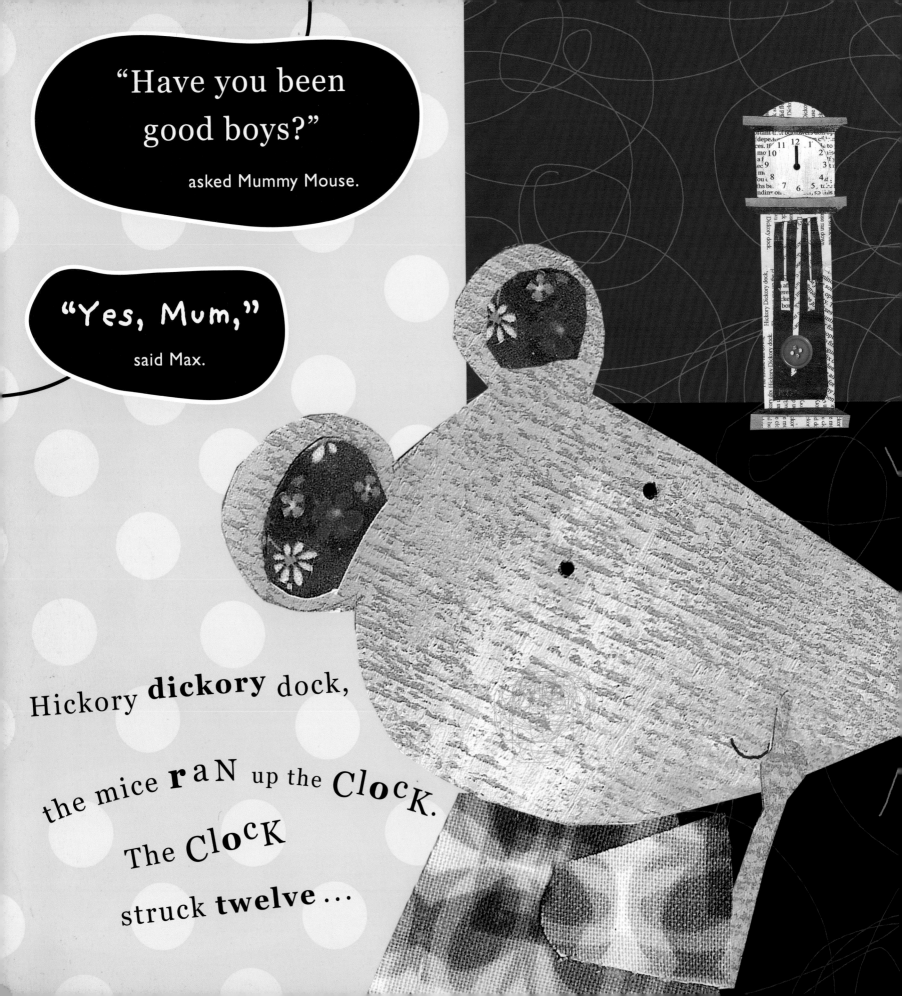

Hickory **dickory** dock.